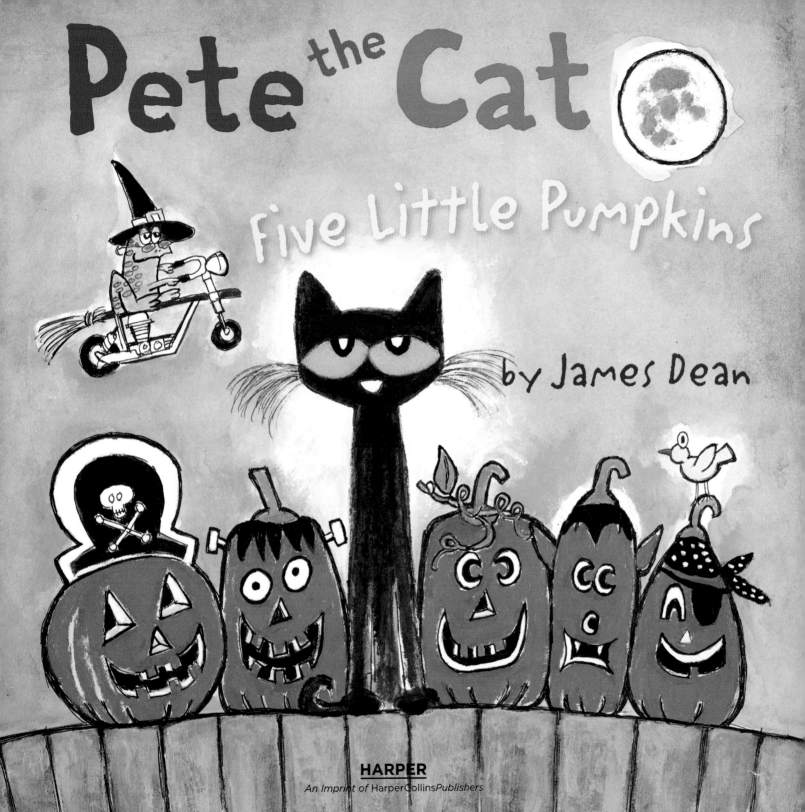

Pete the Cat

Five Little Pumpkins

by James Dean

HARPER

An Imprint of HarperCollinsPublishers

Pete the Cat: Five Little Pumpkins
Copyright © 2015 by James Dean
All rights reserved. Printed in the United States of America.
No part of this book may be used or reproduced in any manner whatsoever without written
permission except in the case of brief quotations embodied in critical articles and reviews.
For information address HarperCollins Children's Books, a division of HarperCollins Publishers,
195 Broadway, New York, NY 10007.
www.harpercollinschildrens.com
Library of Congress Control Number: 2015933437
ISBN 978-0-06-230418-6
Typography by Jeanne L. Hogle
16 17 18 19   PC   10 9 8 7 6 5 4

First Edition

Five little pumpkins

sitting on a gate. The first one said,

The second one said,

"There are witches in the air."

The third one said,
"But we don't care."

The fourth one said,

"Let's run and run and run."

The fifth one said,

Oohh oohh went the wind,

and out went the lights,

and the five little pumpkins

rolled out of sight.